We keep a Pig in the Parlor

Suzanne Bloom

Clarkson N. Potter, Inc./Publishers
DISTRIBUTED BY
CROWN PUBLISHERS, INC., NEW YORK

Some people keep pigs
in a pigpen,
Or out in a field roaming free.
We keep a pig in the parlor.
He sleeps on the settee.

He used to live in the pig barn,
And sit looking out at the field,
Till a plan took shape
For a great escape,
"I want to be free," he squealed.

He fairly flew out of the window,
With a run and a jump and a grunt.
He came down in the mud
With a squishy, soft thud,
It was quite an incredible stunt.

He wandered way out to the pasture
In search of some company.
"I just want a friend to spend time with,"
He said, grinning sheepishly.

We pitched him back in the pig barn,
Tail over snout over heels.
A pen made of pine
Is just fine for a swine,
No matter how loudly he squeals.

Outside he heard quizzical quacking
And finding a large enough crack
Between two loose boards
That rattled like gourds,
He squeezed himself out of that shack.

The zucchini and peas looked so tempting
And the broccoli grew in great clumps.
His tummy felt ever so empty.
He ate everything but the stumps.

FEED

You know, pig, you're driving me crazy.
Why are you doing this stuff?
The garden and barn are a terrible mess.
Enough is enough is enough!"

He looked at me sadly and mumbled,
"I'm sorry I've been such a pest."

Then he snorted and said,

"I detest a straw bed,

Corn that's unpopped,

Supper called slop,

Mud on my face,

That ramshackle place.

It makes me disgruntled, at best.

Besides," he said, "I'm so lonesome,"
And he rested his head on my knee.
As I hugged him I had an idea.
"Piggy, cheer up. Follow me."

So, we keep our pig in the parlor;
He sleeps on the settee.
We watch TV,
Have popcorn and tea
As cozy as we can be.

To Fred, Noah, and Jesse

With special thanks to
Daniel and Cathy

Published by Clarkson N. Potter, Inc., 225 Park Avenue South, New York, New York 10003, and represented in Canada by the Canadian MANDA Group.

CLARKSON N. POTTER, POTTER, and colophon are trademarks of Clarkson N. Potter, Inc.

Manufactured in Italy.

Library of Congress Cataloging-in-Publication Data

Bloom, Suzanne, 1950–
We keep a pig in the parlor.

Summary: A farmer finds a new home for a pig who dislikes living in a barn, sleeping on straw, and eating unpopped corn.
[1. Pigs—Fiction. 2. Farm life—Fiction. 3. Stories in rhyme] I. Title.
PZ8.3.B59836We 1988 [E] 87-29070
ISBN 0-517-56829-2

10 9 8 7 6 5 4 3 2 1

First Edition

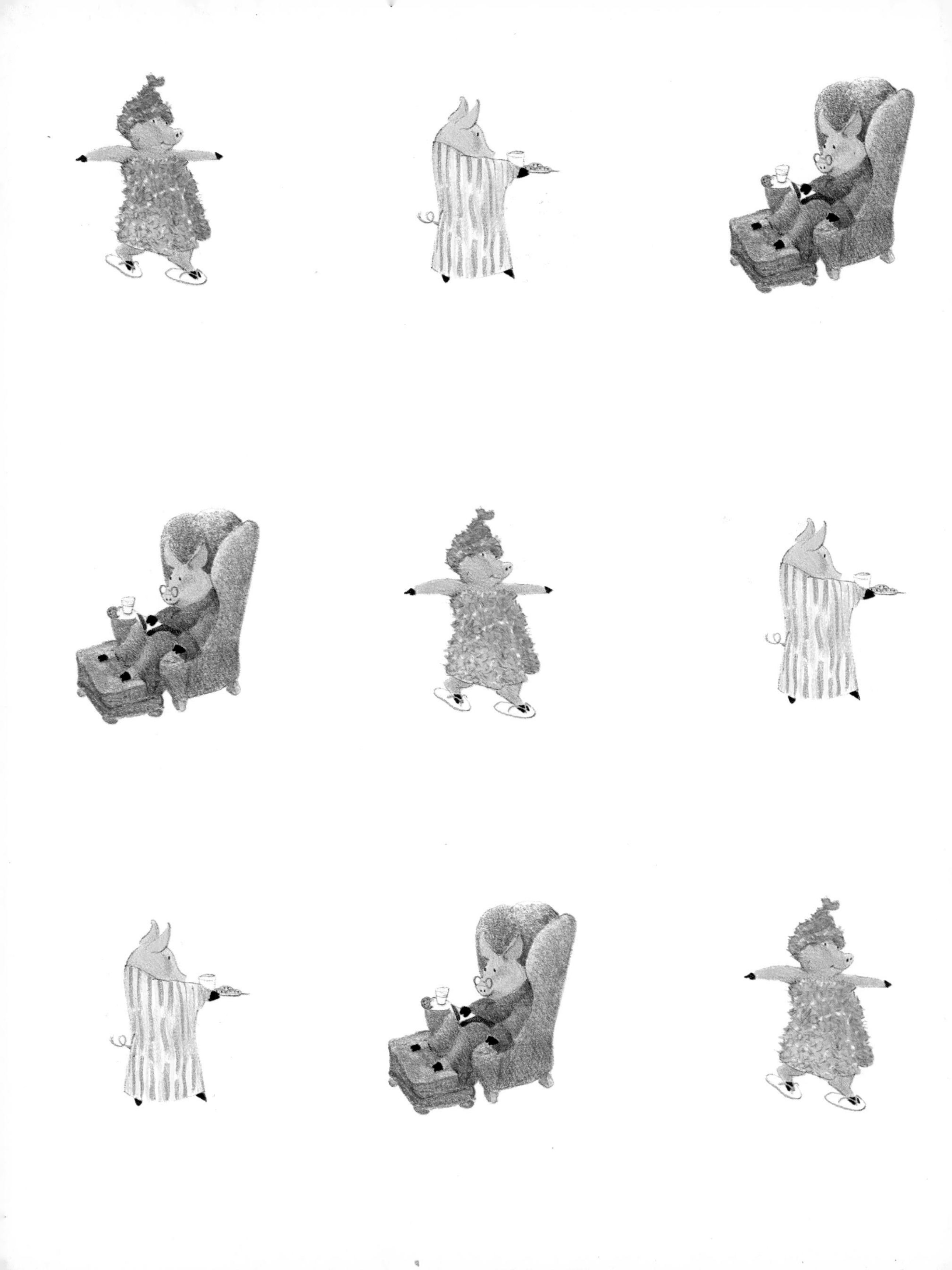